For Alexander with love.
The reason I do all that I do.

 www.dracoviridi.com

Draco Viridi Publication
www.dracoviridi.com | info@dracoviridi.com

First published 2019
© Text and illustration copyright - Suzanne Younan 2019
The moral right of the author has been asserted.

ISBN 978-988-79590-0-7

Typeset and designed by Steffan Leyshon-Jones / urbandecoy.co
Printed and bound by The Green Pagoda Press Ltd, Hong Kong

Printed on Cocoon Silk 100% recycled paper

THE GREEN DRAGON

Written by Suzanne Younan

Illustrated by Caroline Lewington

The Green Dragon was an amazing creature. He was beautiful, strong, kind and very caring. Everything you'd think a dragon wouldn't be.

His name was Willy.

Willy was special in many ways.

One way was his age. Unbelievably, he was more than 100 years old.

Can you imagine being that old? Willy might have been 100 years old – but he wasn't actually 'old'. He was in his prime for a dragon!

Willy the Green Dragon lived in
Hong Kong and loved to spend
his time swimming and flying
around the islands.

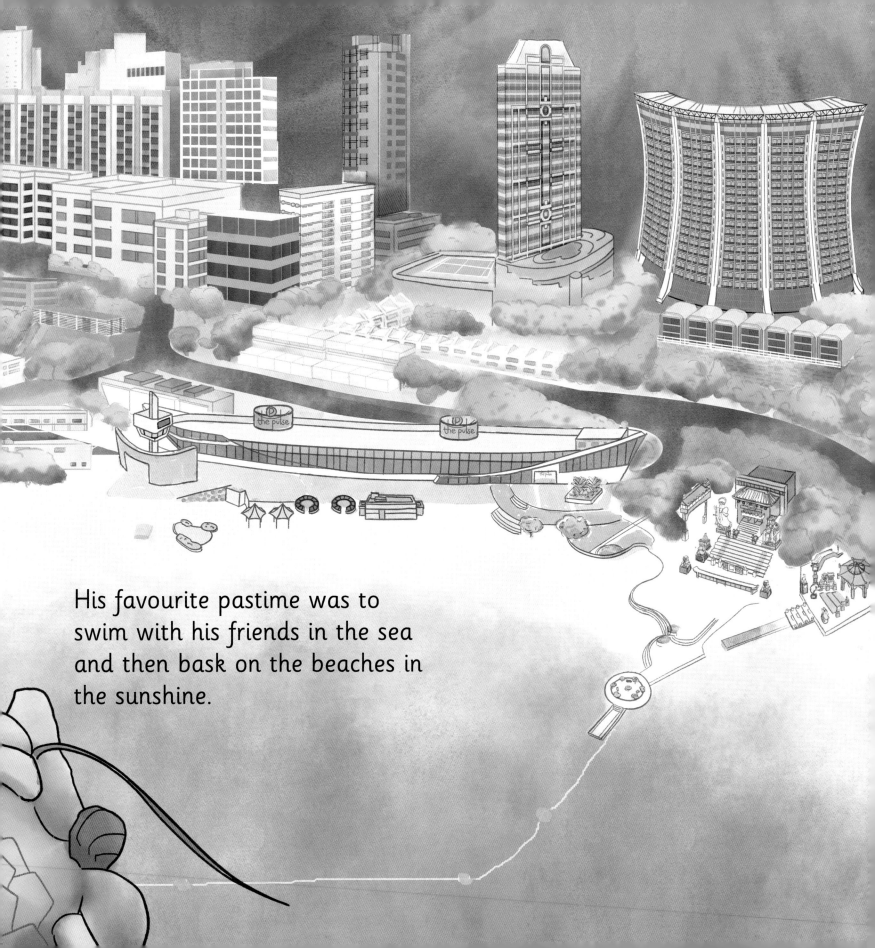

His favourite pastime was to swim with his friends in the sea and then bask on the beaches in the sunshine.

But, recently, life had been difficult for Willy. Times had changed – and not for the better...

Willy had started to notice that people were not so caring about their environment. People were so, so busy and often did what was easiest, not what was best.

Willy found that if he wanted to sunbathe on the beach, he often had to clean it first.

It just wasn't pleasant anymore.

There was a lot of rubbish everywhere. Single-use plastic bottles, plastic bags and plastic straws. They were useful for a very short while and were then thrown away.

Not only was there rubbish on the beach, it was in his beautiful sea.

But Willy had many friends and his friends made him happy. Let me tell you about some of Willy the Green Dragon's friends.

Pearl the Pink Dolphin was a very special friend to Willy.

When Willy was feeling blue, Pearl talked straight and helped him realise what a lucky dragon he really was.

Willy valued Pearl's friendship.

She always knew how to leave him with love in his heart.

One particular morning, Willy was feeling a little down in the mouth about his beautiful scales. They didn't gleam quite as brilliantly as they had before. He decided to find Pearl.

Maybe a game of hide-and-seek would cheer him up.

Pearl wasn't where he normally found her in the waters around Lantau. Willy searched and searched for her. But just when he was about to give up, Willy found Pearl looking unwell.

'Whatever is the matter, Pearl?' Willy said, forgetting his own problem instantly.

'I'm feeling rather ill, Willy,' Pearl replied. 'I ate something bad.'

'Can I help at all, Pearl?' Willy enquired.

'I don't think so, Willy. I made a silly mistake today. A mistake I've been trying to avoid every day of my life', said Pearl.

'I was swimming around, catching some breakfast and quite unexpectedly I sucked down a blue plastic bag. My tummy hurts so, so much. I don't think I can play today. I'm sorry.'

Willy felt helpless. He tried to make Pearl feel better, but whatever he did, her pain would not go away. He wished her well and continued with his day.

I know, thought Willy, I'll go to the turtle beach and see if I can see my friend Myrtle! And off he swam.

Myrtle the Turtle was his cheekiest friend ever. She always saw the positive in everything and liked to tell a lot of jokes. Willy loved to visit her to lift his mood.

After he had been swimming for a while, he rose from the water and flew over the mountains before splashing down again on the edge of the turtle beach on the far side of Lamma Island.

As Willy expected, Myrtle was there – but she did not look like his Myrtle at all!

Her face was very sad.

'Whatever is the matter, Myrtle?' asked Willy.

'Oh, Willy, I'm so sad and upset,' said Myrtle. I was sunning myself on our favourite beach and saw some interesting things washing backwards and forwards in the foam. I had to go and investigate!'

'The next thing I knew, I had something horrible stuck up my nose. I tried and I tried but I could not get it out. My mum tried, and some other turtle friends also. But they poked so hard to remove it that I ended up with a big nose bleed. I just don't feel like playing now. I'm sorry, Willy.'

What Myrtle didn't realise was that she'd had a plastic drinking straw stuck in her nostril. This was truly a disaster.

By now, Willy was feeling even more unhappy. His two best friends were too ill to play with him and cheer him up. And even worse, Pearl and Myrtle had been hurt by plastic that had been thrown in the ocean. Things were getting bad.

Willy wished Myrtle better, blew her a kiss and swam off.

During his onward journey, Willy heard his friend Eddy the Egret flying above him.

'Squawk! Squawk, squawk!!'

It didn't sound good to Willy.

'Eddy, Eddy, are you alright? Whatever is the matter?'

'Oh Willy, I feel horribly sick. I left home in the Mai Po marshes this morning for a little flying and a change of scene when I saw some amazing looking lunch floating in the water. Just bobbing around! Delicious! I thought. I tucked right in,' said Eddy.

'But it wasn't long until I realised this didn't taste good at all and ever since my tummy has been feeling sore. I'm sorry, Willy, I can't stop to chat. I must go home and have a rest.'

And with that, Eddy was gone.

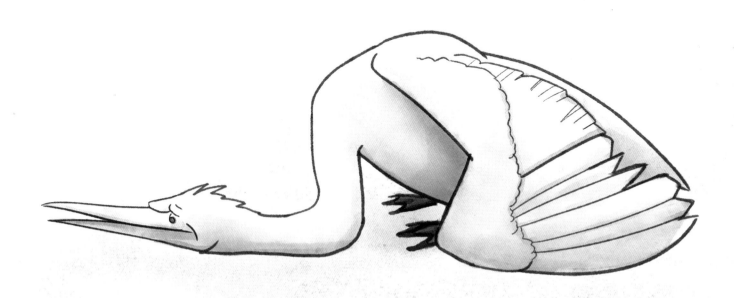

Willy was now growing very concerned. Eddy had eaten some small pieces of styrofoam from a takeaway lunchbox that had washed into the marshes.

With no one to cheer him up, Willy decided he would go back home to the rocks near Stanley on the south side of Hong Kong Island.

Then the unimaginable happened. Willy couldn't swim anymore. Something was wrong. He tried to fly. He couldn't fly either.

He looked back at his beautiful scales and saw that a number of plastic bags had wedged in them and were wrapped around his wings. He started to panic.

Willy tried with all his might to struggle to shore. He was feeling very scared indeed.

Little by little, Willy moved closer to the shore until finally, he flopped, exhausted, onto the sand.

Then he saw that all around him were dead fish. Willy thought his heart would break. This was too much. These beautiful fish had been affected by the pollution in the water, too.

Willy started to cry big, fat tears.

Through his tears, Willy could see a young boy playing on the beach. His parents were busy preparing a family picnic.

In all his 100 years, Willy had avoided people. It wasn't that he was scared or shy, he just felt better with his friends from the sea.

But Willy was too tired to do anything but lie on the beach.

He was safe and he was not worried about the boy.

But soon, the little boy approached him. He wasn't scared of Willy either.

'Hello,' said the boy.

'Hi…,' said Willy, very wearily.

'What's your name?' asked the boy.

'I'm Willy. Willy the Green Dragon. Who are you?'

'I'm Leo. Are you OK?' asked the kind boy.

'Not really,' replied Willy. I have something stuck in my scales and I can't move my wings very well. I was afraid I would drown in the sea.'

'I will help you,' said the boy, bravely.

And with that the little boy gently and slowly pulled out the plastic bags that had tangled in Willy's scales and wings.

Leo's kindness made Willy feel comfortable, so he began to tell the boy about his day. About Pearl, Myrtle and Eddy, and how the plastic in the sea had made them ill.

Leo listened in silence and thought about all that Willy told him.

'This is terrible,' he said, emotionally. 'This has to stop! Our wonderful sea creatures and our beautiful islands are in great danger!'

'I must do something to help!'

The sun began to set. Leo went back to his parents and Willy flew home with a promise to meet Leo again.

But something had changed for Leo.
He had been touched by Willy and his
story. Willy had opened his eyes wide to
the problem Hong Kong was facing. Leo
vowed to make changes and tell everyone
he could about the danger of single-use
plastics.

Before long Leo had involved his
school. He told all the students
with the passion in his heart of
the damage plastic was doing.

With the help of his parents and teachers, he organised beach clean-ups. He said 'NO' to straws at every restaurant. He started to carry his own water bottle. He never used plastic bags, cutlery or plates… He changed his life and the life of others around him, completely. He had decided to reduce the plastic in his life to help save the sea creatures.

He was one little boy who made a change in his world. Imagine what YOU could do in your world, too!

This story was written to touch the hearts of young children and raise awareness to the dangers of plastic pollution in the sea and on land. Although this book is specific to Hong Kong, it can be relevant to anywhere in the world. Sadly, there is a lot to be done.

When you read this book to a child, please include a discussion afterwards:
- How did the story make you feel?
- What are the dangers you see with regard to single-use-plastic pollution?
- How can you make a difference?
- What can you do as a family to reduce single-use plastics in your daily life?

Did you know that Hong Kong throws away 5.2 million plastic bottles EVERY DAY?

We must focus on reduction, not just recycling.

Changes you can make in your life to make a better world:

In the kitchen
- Install a water filter. Stop buying plastic bottles.
- Replace cling film with wax paper.

In the bathroom
- Use bamboo toothbrushes. Ditch the plastic toothbrushes!
- Use a shampoo bar.

Out and about
- Carry a shopping bag with you at all times. Don't use plastic carrier bags.
- Use a refillable water bottle. Use water fountains when you are out and about.
- Say 'No' to plastic straws in your drinks.
- Ask your family to carry their own coffee cups and reusable containers when buying takeaway foods, just like the old days!

Please go to the Draco Viridi web site for a more extensive list of changes you can make for our planet.

www.dracoviridi.com/makethechange

Make the change.
Love your children.
Love the planet.